AN
CA

LIZZIE BORDEN

PENGUIN BOOKS

PENGUIN BOOKS

Published by the Penguin Group. Penguin Books Ltd, 27 Wrights Lane, London
W8 5TZ, England. Penguin Books USA Inc., 375 Hudson Street, New York,
New York 10014, USA. Penguin Books Australia Ltd, Ringwood, Victoria, Australia.
Penguin Books Canada Ltd, 10 Alcorn Avenue, Toronto, Ontario, Canada M4V 3B2.
Penguin Books (NZ) Ltd, 182 – 190 Wairau Road, Auckland 10, New Zealand · Penguin
Books Ltd, Registered Offices: Harmondsworth, Middlesex, England · These
stories are from *Collected Stories* by Angela Carter, published by Chatto & Windus
1995. A version of 'Lizzie's Tiger' was first published in *Cosmopolitan* in 1991 and
broadcast on BBC Radio 3. 'The Fall River Axe Murders' originally appeared in *The
London Review of Books* in 1981 under the title 'Mise-en-Scène for Parricide'. This
edition published 1996. Copyright © Angela Carter, 1981, 1991; copyright © the
Estate of Angela Carter, 1995. All rights reserved · The moral right of the author
has been asserted · Typeset by Rowland Phototypesetting Ltd, Bury St Edmunds,
Suffolk. Printed in England by Clays Ltd, St Ives plc · Except in the United States
of America, this book is sold subject to the condition that it shall not, by way of
trade or otherwise, be lent, re-sold, hired out, or otherwise circulated without the
publisher's prior consent in any form of binding or cover other than that in which it
is published and without a similar condition including this condition being imposed
on the subsequent purchaser · 10 9 8 7 6 5 4 3 2 1

CONTENTS

Lizzie's Tiger

When the circus came to town and Lizzie saw the tiger, they were living on Ferry Street, in a very poor way. It was the time of the greatest parsimony in their father's house; everyone knows the first hundred thousand is the most difficult and the dollar bills were breeding slowly, slowly, even if he practised a little touch of usury on the side to prick his cash in the direction of greater productivity. In another ten years' time, the War between the States would provide rich pickings for the coffin-makers, but, back then, back in the Fifties, well – if he had been a praying man, he would have gone down on his knees for a little outbreak of summer cholera or a touch, just a touch, of typhoid. To his chagrin, there had been nobody to bill when he had buried his wife.

For, at that time, the girls were just freshly orphaned. Emma was thirteen, Lizzie four – stern and square, a squat rectangle of a child. Emma parted Lizzie's hair in the middle, stretched it back over each side of her bulging forehead and braided it tight. Emma dressed her, undressed her, scrubbed her night and morning with a damp flannel, and humped the great lump of little girl around in her arms whenever Lizzie would let her, although Lizzie was not a demonstrative child and did not show affection easily, except to the head of the house, and then only when she wanted something. She knew where the power was and, intuitively feminine in spite of her gruff appearance, she knew how to court it.

That cottage on Ferry – very well, it was a slum; but the undertaker lived on unconcerned among the stiff furnishings of his defunct marriage. His bits and pieces would be admired today if they turned up freshly beeswaxed in an antique store, but in those days they were plain old-fashioned, and time would only make them more so in that dreary interior, the tiny house he never mended, eroding clapboard and diseased paint, mildew on the dark wallpaper with a brown pattern like brains, the ominous crimson border round the top of the walls, the sisters sleeping in one room in one thrifty bed.

On Ferry, in the worst part of town, among the dark-skinned Portuguese fresh off the boat with their earrings, flashing teeth and incomprehensible speech, come over the ocean to work the mills whose newly erected chimneys closed in every perspective; every year more chimneys, more smoke, more newcomers, and the peremptory shriek of the whistle that summoned to labour as bells had once summoned to prayer.

The hovel on Ferry stood, or, rather, leaned at a bibulous angle on a narrow street cut across at an oblique angle by another narrow street, all the old wooden homes like an upset cookie jar of broken gingerbread houses lurching this way and that way, and the shutters hanging off their hinges and windows stuffed with old newspapers, and the snagged picket fence and raised voices in unknown tongues and howling of dogs who, since puppyhood, had known of the world only the circumference of their chain. Outside the parlour window were nothing but rows of counterfeit houses that sometimes used to scream.

Such was the anxious architecture of the two girls' early childhood.

A hand came in the night and stuck a poster, showing the head of a tiger, on to a picket fence. As soon as Lizzie saw the poster, she wanted to go to the circus, but Emma had no money, not a cent. The thirteen-year-old was keeping house at that time, the last skivvy just quit with bad words on both sides. Every morning, Father would compute the day's expenses, hand Emma just so much, no more. He was angry when he saw the poster on the fence; he thought the circus should have paid him rental for the use. He came home in the evening, sweet with embalming fluid, saw the poster, purpled with fury, ripped it off, tore it up.

Then it was supper-time. Emma was no great shakes at cookery and Father, dismissing the possibility of another costly skivvy until such time as plague struck, already pondered the cost-efficiency of remarriage; when Emma served up her hunks of cod, translucently uncooked within, her warmed-over coffee and a dank loaf of baker's bread, it almost put him in a courting mood, but that is not to say his meal improved his temper. So that, when his youngest climbed kitten-like upon his knee and, lisping, twining her tiny fingers in his gunmetal watch-chain, begged small change for the circus, he answered her with words of unusual harshness, for he truly loved this last daughter, whose obduracy recalled his own.

Emma unhandily darned a sock.

'Get that child to bed before I lose my temper!'

Emma dropped the sock and scooped up Lizzie, whose mouth set in dour lines of affront as she was borne off. The square-jawed scrap, deposited on the rustling straw mattress – oat straw, softest and cheapest – sat where she had been dropped and stared at the dust in a sunbeam. She seethed with resentment. It was moist midsummer, only six o'clock and still bright day outside.

She had a will of iron, this one. She swung her feet on to the stool upon which the girls climbed down out of bed, thence to the floor. The kitchen door stood open for air behind the screen door. From the parlour came the low murmur of Emma's voice as she read *The Providence Journal* aloud to Father.

Next-door's lean and famished hound launched itself at the fence in a frenzy of yapping that concealed the creak of Lizzie's boots on the back porch. Unobserved, she was off – off and away! – trotting down Ferry Street, her cheeks pink with self-reliance and intent. She would not be denied.

The circus! The word tinkled in her head with a red sound, as if it might signify a profane church.

'That's a tiger,' Emma had told her as, hand in hand, they inspected the poster on their fence.

'A tiger is a big cat,' Emma added instructively.

How big a cat?

A *very* big cat.

A dumpy, red-striped, regular cat of the small, domestic variety greeted Lizzie with a raucous mew from atop a gatepost as she stumped determinedly along Ferry Street; our cat, Ginger, whom Emma, in a small ecstasy of sentimental whimsy presaging that of her latter protracted spinsterhood, would sometimes call Miss Ginger, or even Miss Ginger Cuddles. Lizzie, however, sternly ignored Miss Ginger Cuddles. Miss Ginger Cuddles sneaked. The cat put out a paw as Lizzie brushed past, as if seeking to detain her, as if to suggest she took second thoughts as to her escapade, but, for all the apparent decision with which Lizzie put one firm foot before the other, she had not the least idea where the circus might be and would not have got there at all without the help of a gaggle of ragged Irish children from Corkey Row, who happened by in the company of a lean, black and tan, barking dog of unforeseen breed that had *this* much in common with Miss Ginger Cuddles, it could go whither it pleased.

This free-ranging dog with its easy-going grin took a fancy to Lizzie and, yapping with glee, danced around the little figure in the white pinafore as it marched along. Lizzie reached out to pat its head. She was a fearless girl.

The child-gang saw her pet their dog and took a fancy to her for the same reason as crows settle on one particular tree. Their wild smiles circled round her. 'Going to the circus, are ye? See the clown and the ladies dancing?' Lizzie knew nothing about clowns and dancers, but she nodded, and one boy took hold of one hand, another of the other, so they raced her off between them. They soon saw her little legs could not keep up their pace, so the ten-year-old put her up on his shoulders where she rode like a lord. Soon they came to a field on the edge of town.

'See the big top?' There was a red and white striped tent of scarcely imaginable proportions, into which you could have popped the entire house on Ferry, and the yard too, with enough room to spare inside for another house, and another – a vast red and white striped tent, with ripping naphtha flares outside and, besides this, all manner of other tents, booths and stalls, dotted about the field, but most of all she was impressed by the great number of people, for it seemed to her that the whole town must be out tonight, yet, when they looked closely at the throng, nowhere at all was anyone who looked like she did, or her father did, or Emma; nowhere that old New England lantern jaw, those ice-blue eyes.

She was a stranger among these strangers, for all here were those the mills had brought to town, the ones with different faces. The plump, pink-cheeked Lancashire mill-hands, with brave red neckerchiefs; the sombre features of the Canucks imbibing fun with characteristic gloom; and the white smiles of the Portuguese, who knew how to enjoy themselves, laughter tripping off their tipsy-sounding tongues.

'Here y'are!' announced her random companions as they dumped her down and, feeling they had amply done their duty by their self-imposed charge, they capered off among the throng, planning, perhaps, to slither under the canvas and so enjoy the shows for free, or even to pick a pocket or two to complete the treat, who knows?

Above the field, the sky now acquired the melting tones of the end of the day, the plush, smoky sunsets unique to these unprecedented industrial cities, sunsets never seen in this world before the Age of Steam that set the mills in motion that made us all modern.

At sunset, the incomparably grave and massive light of New England acquires a monumental, a Roman sensuality; under this sternly voluptuous sky, Lizzie abandoned herself to the unpremeditated smells and never-before-heard noises – hot fat in a vat of frying doughnuts; horse-dung; boiling sugar; frying onions; popping corn; freshly churned earth; vomit; sweat; cries of vendors; crack of rifles from the range; singsong of the white-faced clown, who clattered a banjo, while a woman in pink fleshings danced upon a little stage. Too much for Lizzie to take in at once, too much for Lizzie to take in at all – too rich a feast for her senses, so that she was taken a little beyond herself and felt her head spinning, a vertigo, a sense of profound strangeness overcoming her.

All unnoticeably small as she was, she was taken up by the crowd and tossed about among insensitive shoes and petticoats, too close to the ground to see much else for long; she imbibed the frenetic bustle of the midway through her nose, her ears, her skin that twitched, prickled, heated up with excitement so that she began to colour up in the way she had, her cheeks marked with red, like the marbling on the insides of the family Bible. She found herself swept by the tide of the crowd to a long table where hard cider was sold from a barrel.

The white tablecloth was wet and sticky with spillage and gave forth a dizzy, sweet, metallic odour. An old woman filled tin mugs at the barrel spigot, mug after mug, and threw coins on to other coins into a tin box – splash, chink, clang. Lizzie clung on to the edge of the table to prevent herself being carried away again. Splash, chink, clang. Trade was brisk, so the old woman never turned the spigot off and cider cascaded on to the ground on the other side of the table.

The devil got into Lizzie, then. She ducked down and sneaked in under the edge of the tablecloth, to hide in the resonant darkness and crouch on the crushed grass in fresh mud, as she held out her unobserved hands under the dis-continuous stream from the spigot until she collected two hollowed palmfuls, which she licked up, and smacked her lips. Filled, licked, smacked again. She was so preoccupied with her delicious thievery that she jumped half out of her skin when she felt a living, quivering thing thrust into her neck in that very sensitive spot where her braids divided. Something moist and intimate shoved inquisitively at the nape of her neck.

She craned round and came face to face with a melancholy piglet, decently dressed in a slightly soiled ruff. She courteously filled her palms with cider and offered it to her new acquaintance, who sucked it up eagerly. She squirmed to feel the wet quiver of the pig's curious lips against her hands. It drank, tossed its pink snout, and trotted off out the back way from the table.

Lizzie did not hesitate. She followed the piglet past the dried-cod smell of the cider-seller's skirts. The piglet's tail disappeared beneath a cart piled with fresh barrels that was pulled up behind the stall. Lizzie pursued the engaging piglet to find herself suddenly out in the open again, but this time in an abrupt margin of pitch black and silence. She had slipped out of the circus grounds through a hole in their periphery, and the dark had formed into a huge clot, the night, whilst Lizzie was underneath the table; behind her were the lights, but here only shadowy undergrowth, stirring, and then the call of a night bird.

The pig paused to rootle the earth, but when Lizzie reached out to stroke it, it shook its ears out of its eyes and 9 took off at a great pace into the countryside. However, her attention was immediately diverted from this disappointment by the sight of a man who stood with his back to the lights, leaning slightly forward. The cider-barrel-spigot sound repeated itself. Fumbling with the front of his trousers, he turned round and tripped over Lizzie, because he was a little unsteady on his feet and she was scarcely to be seen among the shadows. He bent down and took hold of her shoulders.

'Small child,' he said, and belched a puff of acridity into her face. Lurching a little, he squatted right down in front of her, so they were on the same level. It was so dark that she could see of his face only the hint of moustache above the pale half-moon of his smile.

'Small girl,' he corrected himself, after a closer look. He did not speak like ordinary folks. He was not from around these parts. He belched again, and again tugged at his trousers. He took firm hold of her right hand and brought it tenderly up between his squatting thighs.

'Small girl, do you know what *this* is for?'

She felt buttons; serge; something hairy; something moist and moving. She didn't mind it. He kept his hand on hers and made her rub him for a minute or two. He hissed between his teeth: 'Kissy, kissy from Missy?'

She *did* mind that and shook an obdurate head; she did not like her father's hard, dry, imperative kisses, and endured them only for the sake of power. Sometimes Emma touched her cheek lightly with unparted lips. Lizzie would allow no more. The man sighed when she shook her head, took her hand away from the crotch, softly folded it up on its fingers and gave her hand ceremoniously back to her.

'Gratuity,' he said, felt in his pocket and flipped her a nickel. Then he straightened up and walked away. Lizzie put the coin in her pinafore pocket and, after a moment's thought, stumped off after the funny man along the still, secret edges of the field, curious as to what he might do next.

But now surprises were going on all around her in the bushes, mewings, squeaks, rustlings, although the funny man paid no attention to them, not even when a stately fat woman rose up under his feet, huge as a moon and stark but for her stays, but for black cotton stockings held up by garters with silk rosettes on them, but for a majestic hat of black leghorn with feathers. The woman addressed the drunken man angrily, in a language with a good many ks in it, but he ploughed on indifferently and Lizzie scuttled unseen after, casting an inquisitive backward glance. She had never seen a woman's naked breasts since she could remember, and this pair of melons jiggled entrancingly as the fat woman shook her fist in the wake of the funny man before she parted her thighs with a wet smack and sank down on her knees again in the grass in which something unseen moaned.

Then a person scarcely as tall as Lizzie herself, dressed

up like a little drummer-boy, somersaulted – head over heels – directly across their paths, muttering to himself as he did so. Lizzie had just the time to see that, although he was small, he was not shaped quite right, for his head seemed to have been pressed into his shoulders with some violence, but then he was gone.

Don't think any of this frightened her. She was not the kind of child that frightens easily.

Then they were at the back of a tent, not the big, striped tent, but another, smaller tent, where the funny man fumbled with the flap much as he had fumbled with his trousers. A bright mauve, ammoniac reek pulsed out from this tent; it was lit up inside like a Chinese lantern and glowed. At last he managed to unfasten and went inside. He did not so much as attempt to close up after him; he seemed to be in as great a hurry as the tumbling dwarf, so she slipped through too, but as soon as she was inside, she lost him, because there were so many other people there.

Feet of customers had worn all the grass from the ground and it had been replaced by sawdust, which soon stuck all over the mudpie Lizzie had become. The tent was lined with cages on wheels, but she could not see high enough to see what was inside them, yet, mixed with the everyday chatter around her, she heard strange cries that did not come from human throats, so she knew she was on the right track.

She saw what could be seen: a young couple, arm in arm,

he whispering in her ear, she giggling; a group of three grinning, gaping youths, poking sticks within the bars; a family that went down in steps of size, a man, a woman, a boy, a girl, a boy, a girl, a boy, a girl, down to a baby of indeterminate sex in the woman's arms. There were many more present, but these were the people she took account of.

The gagging stench was worse than a summer privy and a savage hullabaloo went on all the time, a roaring as if the sea had teeth.

She eeled her way past skirts and trousers and scratched, bare legs of summer boys until she was standing beside the biggest brother of the staircase family at the front of the crowd, but still she could not see the tiger, even if she stood on tiptoe, she saw only wheels and the red and gold base of the cage, whereon was depicted a woman without any clothes, much like the one in the grass outside only without the hat and stockings, and some foliage, with a gilded moon and stars. The brother of the staircase family was much older than she, perhaps twelve, and clearly of the lower class, but clean and respectable-looking, although the entire family possessed that pale, peculiar look characteristic of the mill operatives. The brother looked down and saw a small child in a filthy pinafore peering and straining upwards.

'*Veux-tu voir le grand chat, ma petite?*'

Lizzie did not understand what he said, but she knew 13

what he was saying and nodded assent. Mother looked over
the head of the good baby in the lace bonnet as her son
heaved Lizzie up in his arms for a good look.

'*Les poux . . .*' she warned, but her son paid her no heed.
'*Voilà, ma petite!*'

The tiger walked up and down, up and down; it walked
up and down like Satan walking about the world and it
burned. It burned so brightly, she was scorched. Its tail,
thick as her father's forearm, twitched back and forth at the
tip. The quick, loping stride of the caged tiger; its eyes like
yellow coins of a foreign currency; its round, innocent,
toy-like ears; the stiff whiskers sticking out with an artificial
look; the red mouth from which the bright noise came. It
walked up and down on straw strewn with bloody bones.

The tiger kept its head down; questing hither and thither
though in quest of what might not be told. All its motion
was slung from the marvellous haunches it held so high you
could have rolled a marble down its back, if it would have
let you, and the marble would have run down an oblique
angle until it rolled over the domed forehead on to the floor.
In its hind legs the tense muscles keened and sang. It was
a miracle of dynamic suspension. It reached one end of the
cage in a few paces and whirled around upon itself in one
liquid motion; nothing could be quicker or more beautiful
than its walk. It was all raw, vivid, exasperated nerves. Upon
its pelt it bore the imprint of the bars behind which it lived.

14   The young lad who kept hold of her clung tight as she

lunged forward towards the beast, but he could not stop her clutching the bars of the cage with her little fingers and he tried but he could not dislodge them. The tiger stopped in its track halfway through its mysterious patrol and looked at her. Her pale-blue Calvinist eyes of New England encountered with a shock the flat, mineral eyes of the tiger.

It seemed to Lizzie that they exchanged this cool regard for an endless time, the tiger and herself.

Then something strange happened. The svelte beast fell to its knees. It was as if it had been subdued by the presence of this child, as if this little child of all the children in the world, might lead it towards a peaceable kingdom where it need not eat meat. But only 'as if'. All we could see was, it knelt. A crackle of shock ran through the tent; the tiger was acting out of character.

Its mind remained, however, a law unto itself. We did not know what it was thinking. How could we?

It stopped roaring. Instead it started to emit a rattling purr. Time somersaulted. Space diminished to the field of attractive force between the child and the tiger. All that existed in the whole world now were Lizzie and the tiger.

Then, oh! then . . . it came towards her, as if she were winding it to her on an invisible string by the exercise of pure will. I cannot tell you how much she loved the tiger, nor how wonderful she thought it was. It was the power of her love that forced it to come to her, on its knees, like a penitent. It dragged its pale belly across the dirty straw   15 towards the bars where the little soft creature hung by its hooked fingers. Behind it followed the serpentine length of its ceaselessly twitching tail.

There was a wrinkle in its nose and it buzzed and rumbled and they never took their eyes off one another, though neither had the least idea what the other meant.

The boy holding Lizzie got scared and pummelled her little fists, but she would not let go a grip as tight and senseless as that of the newborn.

Crack! The spell broke.

The world bounded into the ring.

A lash cracked round the tiger's carnivorous head, and a glorious hero sprang into the cage brandishing in the hand that did not hold the whip a three-legged stool. He wore fawn breeches, black boots, a bright red jacket frogged with gold, a tall hat. A dervish, he; he beckoned, crouched, pointed with the whip, menaced with the stool, leaped and twirled in a brilliant ballet of mimic ferocity, the dance of the Taming of the Tiger, to whom the tamer gave no chance to fight at all.

The great cat unpeeled its eyes off Lizzie's in a trice, rose up on its hind legs and feinted at the whip like our puss Ginger feints at a piece of paper dangled from a string. It batted at the tamer with its enormous paws, but the whip continued to confuse, irritate and torment it and, what with the shouting, the sudden, excited baying of the crowd, the dreadful confusion of the signs surrounding it, habitual custom, a lifetime's training, the tiger whimpered, laid back its ears and scampered away from the whirling man to an obscure corner of the stage, there to cower, while its flanks heaved, the picture of humiliation.

Lizzie let go of the bars and clung, mudstains and all, to her young protector for comfort. She was shaken to the roots by the attack of the trainer upon the tiger and her four-year-old roots were very near the surface.

The tamer gave his whip a final, contemptuous ripple around his adversary's whiskers that made it sink its huge head on the floor. Then he placed one booted foot on the tiger's skull and cleared his throat for speech. He was a hero. He was a tiger himself, but even more so, because he was a man.

'Ladies and gentlemen, boys and girls, this incomparable TIGER known as the Scourge of Bengal, and brought alive-oh to Boston from its native jungle but three short months before this present time, now, at my imperious command, offers you a perfect imitation of docility and obedience. But do not let the brute deceive you. Brute it was, and brute it remains. Not for nothing did it receive the soubriquet of Scourge for, in its native habitat, it thought nothing of consuming a dozen brown-skinned heathen for its breakfast and following up with a couple of dozen more for dinner!'

A pleasing shudder tingled through the crowd.

'This tiger,' and the beast whickered ingratiatingly when 17 he named it, 'is the veritable incarnation of blood lust and fury; in a single instant, it can turn from furry quiescence into three hundred pounds, yes, three hundred POUNDS of death-dealing fury.

'The tiger is the cat's revenge.'

Oh, Miss Ginger, Miss Ginger Cuddles, who sat mewing censoriously on the gatepost as Lizzie passed by; who would have thought you seethed with such resentment!

The man's voice dropped to a confidential whisper and Lizzie, although she was in such a state, such nerves, recognized this was the same man as the one she had met behind the cider stall, although now he exhibited such erect mastery, not a single person in the tent would have thought he had been drinking.

'What is the nature of the bond between us, between the Beast and Man? Let me tell you. It is fear. Fear! Nothing but fear. Do you know how insomnia is the plague of the tamer of cats? How all night long, every night, we pace our quarters, impossible to close our eyes for brooding on what day, what hour, what moment the fatal beast will choose to strike?

'Don't think I cannot bleed, or that they have not wounded me. Under my clothes, my body is a palimpsest of scars, scar upon scar. I heal only to be once more broken open. No skin of mine that is not scar tissue. And I am always afraid, always; all the time in the ring, in the cage, now, this moment – this very moment, boys and girls, ladies and gentlemen, you see before you a man in the grip of mortal fear.

'Here and now I am in terror of my life.

'At this moment I am in this cage within a perfect death trap.'

Theatrical pause.

'But,' and here he knocked the tiger's nose with his whipstock, so that it howled with pain and affront, 'but . . .' and Lizzie saw the secret frog he kept within his trousers shift a little, '. . . BUT I'm not half so scared of the big brute as it is of me!'

He showed his red maw in a laugh.

'For I bring to bear upon its killer instinct a rational man's knowledge of the power of fear. The whip, the stool, are instruments of bluff with which I create his fear in my arena. In my cage, among my cats, I have established a hierarchy of FEAR and among my cats you might well say I am TOP DOG, because I know that all the time they want to kill me, that is their project, that is their intention . . . but as for them, they just don't know what I might do next. No, sir!'

As if enchanted by the notion, he laughed out loud again, but by now the tiger, perhaps incensed by the unexpected blow on the nose, rumbled out a clear and incontrovertible message of disaffection and, with a quick jerk of its sculptured head, flung the man's foot away so that, caught off-balance, he half toppled over. And then the tiger was no longer a thing of stillness, of hard edges and clear outlines, but a whiz of black and red, maw and canines, in the air. On him.

The crowd immediately bayed.

But the tamer, with enormous presence of mind, seeing as how he was drunk, and, in the circumstances, with almost uncanny physical agility, bounced backwards on his boot-heels and thrust the stool he carried in his left hand into the fierce tiger's jaws, leaving the tiger worrying, gnawing, destroying the harmless thing, as a ragged black boy quickly unlatched the cage door and out the tamer leaped, un-scathed, amidst hurrahs.

Lizzie's stunned little face was now mottled all over with a curious reddish-purple, with the heat of the tent, with passion, with the sudden access of enlightenment.

To see the rest of the stupendous cat act, the audience would have had to buy another ticket for the Big Top, besides the ticket for the menagerie, for which it had already paid, so, reluctant on the whole to do that, in spite of the promise of clowns and dancing ladies, it soon got bored with watching the tiger splintering the wooden stool, and drifted off.

'*Eh bien, ma petite,*' said her boy-nurse to her in a sweet, singsong, crooning voice. '*Tu as vu la bête! La bête du cau-chemar!*'

The baby in the lace bonnet had slept peacefully through all this, but now began to stir and mumble. Its mother
nudged her husband with her elbow.

'On va, Papa?'

The crooning, smiling boy brought his bright pink lips down on Lizzie's forehead for a farewell kiss. She could not bear that; she struggled furiously and shouted to be put down. With that, her cover broke and she burst out of her disguise of dirt and silence; half the remaining gawpers in the tent had kin been bleakly buried by her father, the rest owed him money. She was the most famous daughter in all Fall River.

'Well, if it ain't Andrew Borden's little girl! What are they Canucks doing with little Lizzie Borden?'

The Fall River Axe Murders

Lizzie Borden with an axe
Gave her father forty whacks
When she saw what she had done
She gave her mother forty-one.

Children's rhyme

Early in the morning of the fourth of August, 1892, in Fall River, Massachusetts.

Hot, hot, hot . . . very early in the morning, before the factory whistle, but, even at this hour, everything shimmers and quivers under the attack of white, furious sun already high in the still air.

Its inhabitants have never come to terms with these hot, humid summers – for it is the humidity more than the heat that makes them intolerable; the weather clings like a low fever you cannot shake off. The Indians who lived here first had the sense to take off their buckskins when hot weather came and sit up to their necks in ponds; not so the descendants of the industrious, self-mortifying saints who imported the Protestant ethic wholesale into a country intended for the siesta and are proud, proud! of flying in the face of nature. In most latitudes with summers like these, everything slows down, then. You stay all day in penumbra behind drawn blinds and closed shutters; you wear clothes loose enough to make your own breeze to cool yourself when you infrequently move. But the ultimate decade of the last century finds us at the high point of hard work, here; all will soon be bustle, men will go out into the furnace of the morning well wrapped up in flannel underclothes, linen shirts, vests and coats and trousers of sturdy woollen cloth, and they garrotte themselves with neckties, too, they think it is so virtuous to be uncomfortable.

And today it is the middle of a heat wave; so early in the morning the mercury has touched the middle eighties, already, and shows no sign of slowing down its headlong ascent.

As far as clothes were concerned, women only appeared to get off more lightly. On this morning, when, after breakfast and the performance of a few household duties, Lizzie Borden will murder her parents, she will, on rising, don a simple cotton frock – but, under that, went a long, starched cotton petticoat; another short, starched cotton petticoat; long drawers; woollen stockings; a chemise; and a whalebone corset that took her viscera in a stern hand and squeezed them very tightly. She also strapped a heavy linen napkin between her legs because she was menstruating.

In all these clothes, out of sorts and nauseous as she was, in this dementing heat, her belly in a vice, she will heat up a flat-iron on a stove and press handkerchiefs with the heated 23 iron until it is time for her to go down to the cellar woodpile to collect the hatchet with which our imagination – 'Lizzie Borden with an axe' – always equips her, just as we always visualize St Catherine rolling along her wheel, the emblem of her passion.

Soon, in just as many clothes as Miss Lizzie wears, if less fine, Bridget, the servant girl, will slop kerosene on a sheet of last night's newspaper crumpled with a stick or two of kindling. When the fire settles down, she will cook breakfast; the fire will keep her suffocating company as she washes up afterwards.

In a serge suit, one look at which would be enough to bring you out in prickly heat, Old Borden will perambulate the perspiring town, truffling for money like a pig until he will return home mid-morning to keep a pressing appointment with destiny.

But nobody here is up and about, yet; it is still early morning, before the factory whistle, the perfect stillness of hot weather, a sky already white, the shadowless light of New England like blows from the eye of God, and the sea, white, and the river, white.

If we have largely forgotten the physical discomforts of the itching, oppressive garments of the past and the corrosive effects of perpetual physical discomfort on the nerves, then we have mercifully forgotten, too, the smells of the past, the domestic odours – ill-washed flesh; infrequently changed underwear; chamber-pots; slop-pails; inadequately plumbed privies; rotting food; unattended teeth; and the streets are no fresher than indoors, the omnipresent acridity of horse piss and dung, drains, sudden stench of old death from butchers' shops, the amniotic horror of the fishmonger.

You would drench your handkerchief with cologne and press it to your nose. You would splash yourself with parma violet so that the reek of fleshly decay you always carried with you was overlaid by that of the embalming parlour. You would abhor the air you breathed.

Five living creatures are asleep in a house on Second Street, Fall River. They compromise two old men and three women. The first old man owns all the women by either marriage, birth or contract. His house is narrow as a coffin and that was how he made his fortune – he used to be an undertaker but he has recently branched out in several directions and all his branches bear fruit of the most fiscally gratifying kind.

But you would never think, to look at his house, that he is a successful and a prosperous man. His house is cramped, comfortless, small and mean – 'unpretentious', you might say, if you were his sycophant – while Second Street itself saw better days some time ago. The Borden house – see 'Andrew J. Borden' in flowing script on the brass plate next to the door – stands by itself with a few scant feet of yard on either side. On the left is a stable, out of use since he sold the horse. In the back lot grow a few pear trees, laden at this season.

On this particular morning, as luck would have it, only one of the two Borden girls sleeps in their father's house. Emma Lenora, his oldest daughter, has taken herself off to nearby New Bedford for a few days, to catch the ocean breeze, and so she will escape the slaughter.

Few of their social class stay in Fall River in the sweating months of June, July and August but, then, few of their social class live on Second Street, in the low part of town where heat gathers like fog. Lizzie was invited away, too, to a summer house by the sea to join a merry band of girls but, as if on purpose to mortify her flesh, as if important business kept her in the exhausted town, as if a wicked fairy spelled her in Second Street, she did not go.

The other old man is some kind of kin of Borden's. He doesn't belong here; he is visiting, passing through, he is a chance bystander, he is irrelevant.

Write him out of the script.

Even though his presence in the doomed house is historically unimpeachable, the colouring of this domestic apocalypse must be crude and the design profoundly simplified for the maximum emblematic effect.

Write John Vinnicum Morse out of the script.

One old man and two of his women sleep in the house on Second Street.

The City Hall clock whirrs and sputters the prolegomena to the first stroke of six and Bridget's alarm clock gives a sympathetic skip and click as the minute-hand stutters on the hour; back the little hammer jerks, about to hit the bell on top of her clock, but Bridget's damp eyelids do not shudder with premonition as she lies in her sticking flannel nightgown under one thin sheet on an iron bedstead, lies on her back, as the good nuns taught her in her Irish girlhood, in case she dies during the night, to make less trouble for the undertaker.

She is a good girl, on the whole, although her temper is sometimes uncertain and then she will talk back to the missus, sometimes, and will be forced to confess the sin of impatience to the priest. Overcome by heat and nausea – for everyone in the house is going to wake up sick today – she will return to this little bed later in the morning. While she snatches a few moments' rest, upstairs, all hell will be let loose, downstairs.

A rosary of brown glass beads, a cardboard-backed colour print of the Virgin bought from a Portuguese shop, a fly-blown photograph of her solemn mother in Donegal – these lie or are propped on the mantelpiece that, however sharp the Massachusetts winter, has never seen a lit stick. A banged tin trunk at the foot of the bed holds all Bridget's worldly goods.

There is a stiff chair beside the bed with, upon it, a candlestick, matches, the alarm clock that resounds the room with a dyadic, metallic clang, for it is a joke between Bridget and her mistress that the girl could sleep through anything, *anything*, and so she needs the alarm as well as all the factory whistles that are just about to blast off, just this very second about to blast off . . .

A splintered deal washstand holds the jug and bowl she never uses; she isn't going to lug water up to the third floor just to wipe herself down, is she? Not when there's water enough in the kitchen sink.

Old Borden sees no necessity for baths. He does not believe in total immersion. To lose his natural oils would be to rob his body.

A frameless square of mirror reflects in corrugated waves a cracked, dusty soap dish containing a quantity of black metal hairpins.

On bright rectangles of paper blinds move the beautiful shadows of the pear trees.

Although Bridget left the door open a crack in forlorn hopes of coaxing a draught into the room, all the spent heat of the previous day has packed itself tightly into her attic. A dandruff of spent whitewash flakes from the ceiling where a fly drearily whines.

The house is thickly redolent of sleep, that sweetish, clinging smell. Still, all still; in all the house nothing moving except the droning fly. Stillness on the staircase. Stillness pressing against the blinds. Stillness, mortal stillness in the room below, where Master and Mistress share the matrimonial bed.

Were the drapes open or the lamp lit, one could better
observe the differences between this room and the austerity

of the maid's room. Here is a carpet splashed with vigorous flowers, even if the carpet is of the cheap and cheerful variety; there are mauve, ochre and harsh cerise flowers on the wallpaper, even though the wallpaper was old when the Bordens arrived in the house. A dresser with another distorting mirror; no mirror in this house does not take your face and twist it. On the dresser, a runner embroidered with forget-me-nots; on the runner, a bone comb missing three teeth and lightly threaded with grey hairs, a hairbrush backed with ebonized wood, and a number of lace mats underneath small china boxes holding safety-pins, hairnets etc. The little hairpiece that Mrs Borden attaches to her balding scalp for daytime wear is curled up like a dead squirrel. But of Borden's male occupation of this room there is no trace because he has a dressing room of his own, through *that* door, on the left . . .

What about the other door, the one next to it?

It leads to the back stairs.

And that yet other door, partially concealed behind the head of the heavy, mahogany bed?

If it were not kept securely locked, it would take you into Miss Lizzie's room.

One peculiarity of this house is the number of doors the rooms contain and, a further peculiarity, how all these doors are always locked. A house full of locked doors that open only into other rooms with other locked doors, for, upstairs and downstairs, all the rooms lead in and out of one another 29 like a maze in a bad dream. It is a house without passages. There is no part of the house that has not been marked as some inmate's personal territory; it is a house with no shared, no common spaces between one room and the next. It is a house of privacies sealed as close as if they had been sealed with wax on a legal document.

The only way to Emma's room is through Lizzie's. There is no way out of Emma's room. It is a dead end.

The Bordens' custom of locking all the doors, inside and outside, dates from a time, a few years ago, shortly before Bridget came to work for them, when the house was burgled. A person unknown came through the side door while Borden and his wife had taken one of their rare trips out together; he had loaded her into a trap and set out for the farm they owned at Swansea to ensure his tenant was not bilking him. The girls stayed at home in their rooms, napping on their beds or repairing ripped hems or sewing loose buttons more securely or writing letters or contemplating acts of charity among the deserving poor or staring vacantly into space.

I can't imagine what else they might do.

What the girls do when they are on their own is unimaginable to me.

Emma is more mysterious by far than Lizzie, for we know much less about her. She is a blank space. She has no life. The door from her room leads only into the room of her sister.

'Girls' is, of course, a courtesy term. Emma is well into her forties, Lizzie in her thirties, but they did not marry and so live in their father's house, where they remain in a fictive, protracted childhood.

While the master and the mistress were away and the girls asleep or otherwise occupied, some person or persons unknown tiptoed up the back stairs to the matrimonial bedroom and pocketed Mrs Borden's gold watch and chain, the coral necklace and silver bangle of her remote childhood, and a roll of dollar bills Old Borden kept under clean union suits in the third drawer of the bureau on the left. The intruder attempted to force the lock of the safe, that featureless block of black iron like a slaughtering block or an altar sitting squarely next to the bed on Old Borden's side, but it would have taken a crowbar to penetrate adequately the safe and the intruder tackled it with a pair of nail scissors that were lying handy on the dresser so *that* didn't come off.

Then the intruder pissed and shat on the cover of the Bordens' bed, knocked the clutter of this and that on the dresser to the floor, smashing everything, swept into Old Borden's dressing room there to maliciously assault the funeral coat as it hung in the moth-balled dark of his closet with the self-same nail scissors that had been used on the safe (the nail scissors now split in two and were abandoned on the closet floor), retired to the kitchen, smashed the flour crock and the treacle crock, and then scrawled an obscenity 31 or two on the parlour window with the cake of soap that lived beside the scullery sink.

What a mess! Lizzie stared with vague surprise at the parlour window; she heard the soft bang of the open screen door, swinging idly, although there was no breeze. What was she doing, standing clad only in her corset in the middle of the sitting room? How had she got there? Had she crept down when she heard the screen door rattle? She did not know. She could not remember.

All that happened was: all at once here she is, in the parlour, with a cake of soap in her hand.

She experienced a clearing of the senses and only then began to scream and shout.

'Help! We have been burgled! Help!'

Emma came down and comforted her, as the big sister had comforted the little one since babyhood. Emma it was who cleared from the sitting-room carpet the flour and treacle Lizzie had heedlessly tracked in from the kitchen on her bare feet in her somnambulist trance. But of the missing jewellery and dollar bills no trace could be found.

I cannot tell you what effect the burglary had on Borden. It utterly disconcerted him; he was a man stunned. It violated him, even. He was a man raped. It took away his hitherto unshakeable confidence in the integrity inherent in things.

The burglary so moved them that the family broke its
habitual silence with one another in order to discuss it. They

blamed it on the Portuguese, obviously, but sometimes on the Canucks. If their outrage remained constant and did not diminish with time, the focus of it varied according to their moods, although they always pointed the finger of suspicion at the strangers and newcomers who lived in the gruesome ramparts of the company housing a few squalid blocks away. They did not always suspect the dark strangers exclusively; sometimes they thought the culprit might very well have been one of the mill-hands fresh from saucy Lancashire across the ocean who committed the crime, for a slum land-lord has few friends among the criminal classes.

However, the possibility of a poltergeist occurs to Mrs Borden, although she does not know the word; she knows, however, that her younger stepdaughter is a strange one and could make the plates jump out of sheer spite, if she wanted to. But the old man adores his daughter. Perhaps it is then, after the shock of the burglary, that he decides she needs a change of scene, a dose of sea air, a long voyage, for it was after the burglary he sent her on the grand tour.

After the burglary, the front door and the side door were always locked three times if one of the inhabitants of the house left it for just so much as to go into the yard and pick up a basket of fallen pears when pears were in season or if the maid went out to hang a bit of washing or Old Borden, after supper, took a piss under a tree.

From this time dated the custom of locking all the bed-room doors on the inside when one was on the inside oneself or on the outside when one was on the outside. Old Borden locked his bedroom door in the morning, when he left it, and put the key in sight of all on the kitchen shelf.

The burglary awakened Old Borden to the evanescent nature of private property. He thereafter undertook an orgy of investment. He would forthwith invest his surplus in good brick and mortar, for who can make away with an office block?

A number of leases fell in simultaneously at just this time on a certain street in the downtown area of the city and Borden snapped them up. He owned the block. He pulled it down. He planned the Borden building, an edifice of shops and offices, dark red brick, deep tan stone, with cast-iron detail, from whence, in perpetuity, he might reap a fine harvest of unsaleable rents, and this monument, like that of Ozymandias, would long survive him – and, indeed, stands still, foursquare and handsome, the Andrew Borden Building, on South Main Street.

Not bad for a fish peddler's son, eh?

For, although 'Borden' is an ancient name in New England and the Borden clan between them owned the better part of Fall River, our Borden, Old Borden, these Bordens, did not spring from a wealthy branch of the family. There were Bordens and Bordens and he was the son of a man who sold fresh fish in a wicker basket from house to house to house. Old Borden's parsimony was bred of poverty but learned to thrive best on property, for thrift has a different meaning for the poor; they get no joy of it, it is stark necessity to them. Whoever heard of a penniless miser?

Morose and gaunt, this self-made man is one of few pleasures. His vocation is capital accumulation.

What is his hobby?

Why, grinding the faces of the poor.

First, Andrew Borden was an undertaker, and death, recognizing an accomplice, did well by him. In the city of spindles, few made old bones; the little children who laboured in the mills died with especial frequency. When he was an undertaker, no! – it was not true he cut the feet off corpses to fit into a job lot of coffins bought cheap as Civil War surplus! That was a rumour put about by his enemies!

With the profits from his coffins, he bought up a tenement or two and made fresh profit off the living. He bought shares in the mills. Then he invested in a bank or two, so that now he makes a profit on money itself, which is the purest form of profit of all.

Foreclosures and evictions are meat and drink to him. He loves nothing better than a little usury. He is halfway on the road to his first million.

At night, to save the kerosene, he sits in lampless dark. He waters the pear trees with his urine; waste not, want not. As soon as the daily newspapers are done with, he rips them up in geometric squares and stores them in the cellar privy so that they all can wipe their arses with them. He mourns the loss of the good organic waste that flushes down the W C. He would like to charge the very cockroaches in the kitchen rent. And yet he has not grown fat on all this; the pure flame of his passion has melted off his flesh, his skin sticks to his bones out of sheer parsimony. Perhaps it is from his first profession that he has acquired his bearing, for he walks with the stately dignity of a hearse.

To watch Old Borden bearing down the street towards you was to be filled with an instinctual respect for mortality, whose gaunt ambassador he seemed to be. And it made you think, too, what a triumph over nature it was when we rose up to walk on two legs instead of four, in the first place! For he held himself upright with such ponderous assertion it was a perpetual reminder to all who witnessed his progress how it is not *natural* to be upright, that it is a triumph of will over gravity, in itself a transcendence of the spirit over matter.

His spine is like an iron rod, forged, not born, impossible to imagine that spine of Old Borden's curled up in the womb in the big C of the foetus; he walks as if his legs had joints at neither knee nor ankle so that his feet hit the trembling earth like a bailiff pounding a door.

He has a white, chin-strap beard, old-fashioned already in those days. He looks as if he'd gnawed his lips off. He is at peace with his god for he has used his talents as the Good Book says he should.

Yet do not think he has no soft spot. Like Old Lear, his

heart – and, more than that, his cheque-book – is putty in his youngest daughter's hands. On his pinky – you cannot see it, it lies under the covers – he wears a gold ring, not a wedding ring but a high-school ring, a singular trinket for a fabulously misanthropic miser. His youngest daughter gave it to him when she left school and asked him to wear it, always, and so he always does, and will wear it to the grave to which she is going to send him later in the morning of this combustible day.

He sleeps fully dressed in a flannel nightshirt over his long-sleeved underwear, and a flannel nightcap, and his back is turned towards his wife of thirty years, as is hers to his.

They are Mr and Mrs Jack Sprat in person, he tall and gaunt as a hanging judge and she, such a spreading, round little doughball. He is a miser, while she is a glutton, a solitary eater, most innocent of vices and yet the shadow or parodic vice of his, for he would like to eat up all the world, or, failing that, since fate has not spread him a sufficiently large table for his ambitions, he is a mute, inglorious Napoleon, he does not know what he might have done because he never had the opportunity – since he has not access to the entire world, he would like to gobble up the city of Fall River. But she, well, she just gently, continuously stuffs herself, doesn't she; she's always nibbling away at something, at the cud, perhaps.

Not that she gets much pleasure from it, either; no gourmet, she, forever meditating the exquisite difference 37 between a mayonnaise sharpened with a few drops of Orleans vinegar or one pointed up with a squeeze of fresh lemon juice. No. Abby never aspired so high, nor would she ever think to do so even if she had the option; she is satisfied to stick to simple gluttony and she eschews all overtones of the sensuality of indulgence. Since she relishes not one single mouthful of the food she eats, she knows her ceaseless gluttony is no transgression.

Here they lie in bed together, living embodiments of two of the Seven Deadly Sins, but he knows his avarice is no offence because he never spends any money and she knows she is not greedy because the grub she shovels down gives her dyspepsia.

She employs an Irish cook and Bridget's rough-and-ready hand in the kitchen fulfils Abby's every criterion. Bread, meat, cabbage, potatoes – Abby was made for the heavy food that made her. Bridget merrily slaps on the table boiled dinners, boiled fish, cornmeal mush, Indian pudding, johnnycakes, cookies.

But those cookies . . . ah! there you touch on Abby's little weakness. Molasses cookies, oatmeal cookies, raisin cookies. But when she tackles a sticky brownie, oozing chocolate, then she feels a queasy sense of having gone almost too far, that sin might be just around the corner if her stomach did not immediately palpitate like a guilty conscience.

Her flannel nightdress is cut on the same lines as his

nightshirt except for the limp flannel frill round the neck. She weighs two hundred pounds. She is five feet nothing tall. The bed sags on her side. It is the bed in which his first wife died.

Last night, they dosed themselves with castor oil, due to the indisposition that kept them both awake and vomiting the whole night before that; the copious results of their purges brim the chamber-pots beneath the bed. It is fit to make a sewer faint.

Back to back they lie. You could rest a sword in the space between the old man and his wife, between the old man's backbone, the only rigid thing he ever offered her, and her soft, warm, enormous bum. Their purges flailed them. Their faces show up decomposing green in the gloom of the curtained room, in which the air is too thick for flies to move.

The youngest daughter dreams behind the locked door.

Look at the sleeping beauty!

She threw back the top sheet and her window is wide open but there is no breeze, outside, this morning, to shiver deliciously the screen. Bright sun floods the blinds so that the linen-coloured light shows us how Lizzie has gone to bed as for a levée in a pretty, ruffled nightdress of snatched white muslin with ribbons of pastel pink satin threaded through the eyelets of the lace, for is it not the 'naughty Nineties' everywhere but dour Fall River? Don't the gilded steamships of the Fall River Line signify all the squandered luxury of the Gilded Age within their mahogany and chandeliered interiors? But don't they sail *away* from Fall River, to where, elsewhere, it is the Belle Epoque? In New York, Paris, London, champagne corks pop, in Monte Carlo the bank is broken, women fall backwards in a crisp meringue of petticoats for fun and profit, but not in Fall River. Oh, no. So, in the immutable privacy of her bedroom, for her own delight, Lizzie puts on a rich girl's pretty nightdress, although she lives in a mean house, because she is a rich girl, too.

But she is plain.

The hem of her nightdress is rucked up above her knees because she is a restless sleeper. Her light, dry, reddish hair, crackling with static, slipping loose from the night-time plait, crisps and stutters over the square pillow at which she clutches as she sprawls on her stomach, having rested her cheek on the starched pillowcase for coolness' sake at some earlier hour.

Lizzie was not an affectionate diminutive but the name with which she had been christened. Since she would always be known as 'Lizzie', so her father reasoned, why burden her with the effete and fancy prolongation of 'Elizabeth'? A miser in everything, he even cropped off half her name before he gave it to her. So 'Lizzie' it was, stark and unadorned, and she is a motherless child, orphaned at two years old, poor thing.

Now she is two-and-thirty and yet the memory of that

mother she cannot remember remains an abiding source of grief: 'If mother had lived, everything would have been different.'

How? Why? Different in what way? She wouldn't have been able to answer that, lost in a nostalgia for unknown love. Yet how could she have been loved better than by her sister, Emma, who lavished the pent-up treasures of a New England spinster's heart upon the little thing? Different, perhaps, because her natural mother, the first Mrs Borden, subject as she was to fits of sudden, wild, inexplicable rage, might have taken the hatchet to Old Borden on her own account? But Lizzie *loves* her father. All are agreed on that. Lizzie adores the adoring father who, after her mother died, took to himself another wife.

Her bare feet twitch a little, like those of a dog dreaming of rabbits. Her sleep is thin and unsatisfying, full of vague terrors and indeterminate menaces to which she cannot put a name or form once she is awake. Sleep opens within her a disorderly house. But all she knows is, she sleeps badly, and this last, stifling night has been troubled, too, by vague nausea and the gripes of her female pain; her room is harsh with the metallic smell of menstrual blood.

Yesterday evening she slipped out of the house to visit a woman friend. Lizzie was agitated; she kept picking nervously at the shirring on the front of her dress.

'I am afraid . . . that somebody . . . will *do* something,' said Lizzie.

41

'Mrs Borden . . .' and here Lizzie lowered her voice and her eyes looked everywhere in the room except at Miss Russell . . . 'Mrs Borden – oh! will you ever believe? Mrs Borden thinks somebody is trying to *poison* us!'

She used to call her stepmother 'mother', as duty bade, but, after a quarrel about money after her father deeded half a slum property to her stepmother five years before, Lizzie always, with cool scrupulosity, spoke of 'Mrs Borden' when she was forced to speak of her, and called her 'Mrs Borden' to her face, too.

'Last night, Mrs Borden and poor father were so sick! I heard them, through the wall. And, as for me, I haven't felt myself all day, I have felt so strange. So very . . . strange.'

For there were those somnambulist fits. Since a child, she endured occasional 'peculiar spells', as the idiom of the place and time called odd lapses of behaviour, unexpected, involuntary trances, moments of disconnection. Those times when the mind misses a beat. Miss Russell hastened to discover an explanation within reason; she was embarrassed to mention the 'peculiar spells'. Everyone knew there was nothing odd about the Borden girls.

'Something you ate? It must have been something you have eaten. What was yesterday's supper?' solicitously queried kind Miss Russell.

'Warmed-over swordfish. We had it hot for dinner though I could not take much. Then Bridget heated up the leftovers for supper but, again, for myself, I could only get down a forkful. Mrs Borden ate up the remains and scoured her plate with her bread. She smacked her lips but then was sick all night.' (Note of smugness, here.)

'Oh, Lizzie! In all this heat, this dreadful heat! Twice-cooked fish! You know how quickly fish goes off in this heat! Bridget should have known better than to give you twice-cooked fish!'

It was Lizzie's difficult time of the month, too; her friend could tell by a certain haggard, glazed look on Lizzie's face. Yet her gentility forbade her to mention that. But how could Lizzie have got it into her head that the entire household was under siege from malign forces without?

'There have been threats,' Lizzie pursued remorselessly, keeping her eyes on her nervous fingertips. 'So many people, you understand, dislike Father.'

This cannot be denied. Miss Russell politely remained mute.

'Mrs Borden was so very sick she called the doctor in and Father was abusive towards the doctor and shouted at him and told him he would not pay a doctor's bills whilst we had our own good castor oil in the house. He shouted at the doctor and all the neighbours heard and I was so ashamed. There is a man, you see . . .' and here she ducked her head, while her short, pale eyelashes beat on her cheek bones . . . 'such a man, a *dark* man, with the aspect, yes of death upon his face, Miss Russell, a dark man I've seen outside the house at odd, at unexpected hours, early in the morning, late at night, whenever I cannot sleep in this dreadful shade if I raise the blind and peep out, there I see him in the shadows of the pear trees, in the yard, a dark man . . . perhaps he puts poison in the milk, in the mornings, after the milkman fills his can. Perhaps he poisons the ice, when the iceman comes.'

'How long has he been haunting you?' asked Miss Russell, properly dismayed.

'Since . . . the burglary,' said Lizzie and suddenly looked Miss Russell full in the face with a kind of triumph. How large her eyes were; prominent, yet veiled. And her well-manicured fingers went on pecking away at the front of her dress as if she were trying to unpick the shirring.

Miss Russell knew, she just *knew*, this dark man was a figment of Lizzie's imagination. All in a rush, she lost patience with the girl; dark men standing outside her bedroom window, indeed! Yet she was kind and cast about for ways to reassure.

'But Bridget is up and about when the milkman, the iceman call and the whole street is busy and bustling, too; who would dare to put poison in either milk or ice-bucket while half of Second Street looks on? Oh, Lizzie, it is the dreadful summer, the heat, the intolerable heat that's put us all out of sorts, makes us fractious and nervous, makes us sick. So easy to imagine things in this terrible weather, that taints the food and sows worms in the mind . . . I thought you'd planned to go away, Lizzie, to the ocean.

Didn't you plan to take a little holiday, by the sea? Oh, do go! Sea air would blow away these silly fancies!'

Lizzie neither nods nor shakes her head but continues to worry at her shirring. For does she not have important business in Fall River? Only that morning, had she not been down to the drug-store to try to buy some prussic acid herself? But how can she tell kind Miss Russell she is gripped by an imperious need to stay in Fall River and murder her parents?

She went to the drug-store on the corner of Main Street in order to buy prussic acid but nobody would sell it to her, so she came home empty-handed. Had all that talk of poison in the vomiting house put her in mind of poison? The autopsy will reveal no trace of poison in the stomachs of either parent. She did not try to poison them; she only had it in mind to poison them. But she had been unable to buy poison. The use of poison had been denied her; so what can she be planning, now?

'And this dark man,' she pursued to the unwilling Miss Russell, 'oh! I have seen the moon glint upon an *axe*!'

When she wakes up, she can never remember her dreams; she only remembers she slept badly.

Hers is a pleasant room of not ungenerous dimensions, seeing the house is so very small. Besides the bed and the dresser, there is a sofa and a desk; it is her bedroom and also her sitting room and her office, too, for the desk is stacked with account books of the various charitable 45 organizations with which she occupies her ample spare time. The Fruit and Flower Mission, under whose auspices she visits the indigent old in hospital with gifts; the Women's Christian Temperance Union, for whom she extracts signatures for petitions against the Demon Drink; Christian Endeavour, whatever that is – this is the golden age of good works and she flings herself into committees with a vengeance. What would the daughters of the rich do with themselves if the poor ceased to exist?

There is the Newsboys Thanksgiving Dinner Fund; and the Horsetrough Association; and the Chinese Conversion Association – no class nor kind is safe from her merciless charity.

Bureau; dressing-table; closet; bed; sofa. She spends her days in this room, moving between each of these dull items of furniture in a circumscribed, undeviating, planetary round. She loves her privacy, she loves her room, she locks herself up in it all day. A shelf contains a book or two: *Heroes of the Mission Field*, *The Romance of Trade*, *What Katy Did*. On the walls, framed photographs of high-school friends, sentimentally inscribed, with, tucked inside one frame, a picture postcard showing a black kitten peeking through a horseshoe. A watercolour of a Cape Cod seascape executed with poignant amateur incompetence. A monochrome photograph or two of works of art, a Della Robbia madonna and the Mona Lisa; these she bought in the Uffizi and the Louvre respectively when she went to Europe.

Europe!

For don't you remember what Katy did next? The story-book heroine took the steamship to smoky old London, to elegant, fascinating Paris, to sunny, antique Rome and Florence, the story-book heroine sees Europe reveal itself before her like an interesting series of magic-lantern slides on a gigantic screen. All is present and all unreal. The Tower of London; click. Notre Dame; click. The Sistine Chapel; click. Then the lights go out and she is in the dark again.

Of this journey she retained only the most circumspect of souvenirs, that madonna, that Mona Lisa, reproductions of objects of art consecrated by a universal approval of taste. If she came back with a bag full of memories stamped 'Never to be Forgotten', she put the bag away under the bed on which she had dreamed of the world before she set out to see it and on which, at home again, she continued to dream, the dream having been transformed not into lived experience but into memory, which is only another kind of dreaming.

Wistfully: 'When I was in Florence . . .'

But then, with pleasure, she corrects herself: 'When *we* were in Florence . . .'

Because a good deal, in fact most, of the gratification the trip gave her came from having set out from Fall River with a select group of the daughters of respectable and affluent mill-owners. Once away from Second Street, she was able to move comfortably in the segment of Fall River society to which she belonged by right of old name and new money

47

but from which, when she was at home, her father's plentiful personal eccentricities excluded her. Sharing bedrooms, sharing state-rooms, sharing berths, the girls travelled together in a genteel gaggle that bore its doom already upon it, for they were the girls who would not marry, now, and any pleasure they might have obtained from the variety and excitement of the trip was spoiled in advance by the knowledge they were eating up what might have been their own wedding-cake, using up what should have been, if they'd had any luck, their marriage settlements.

All girls pushing thirty, privileged to go out and look at the world before they resigned themselves to the thin condition of New England spinsterhood; but it was a case of look, don't touch. They knew they must not get their hands dirtied or their dresses crushed by the world, while their affectionate companionship en route had a certain steadfast, determined quality about it as they bravely made the best of the second-best.

It was a sour trip, in some ways, sour; and it was a round trip, it ended at the sour place from where it had set out. Home, again; the narrow house, the rooms all locked like those in Bluebeard's castle, and the fat, white stepmother whom nobody loves sitting in the middle of the spider web, she has not budged a single inch while Lizzie was away but she has grown fatter.

This stepmother oppressed her like a spell.

The days open their cramped spaces into other cramped

spaces and old furniture and never anything to look forward to, nothing.

When Old Borden dug in his pocket to shell out for Lizzie's trip to Europe, the eye of God on the pyramid blinked to see daylight, but no extravagance is too excessive for the miser's younger daughter who is the wild card in his house and, it seems, can have anything she wants, play ducks and drakes with her father's silver dollars if it so pleases her. He pays all her dressmakers' bills on the dot and how she loves to dress up fine! She is addicted to dandyism. He gives her each week in pin-money the same as the cook gets for wages and Lizzie gives that which she does not spend on personal adornment to the deserving poor.

He would give his Lizzie anything, anything in the world that lives under the green sign of the dollar.

She would like a pet, a kitten or a puppy, she loves small animals and birds, too, poor, helpless things. She piles high the bird-table all winter. She used to keep some white pouter pigeons in the disused stable, the kind that look like shuttlecocks and go 'vroo croo', soft as a cloud.

Surviving photographs of Lizzie Borden show a face it is difficult to look at as if you knew nothing about her; coming events cast their shadow across her face, or else you see the shadows these events have cast – something terrible, something ominous in this face with its jutting, rectangular jaw and those mad eyes of the New England saints, eyes

that belong to a person who does not listen to you ...
fanatic's eyes, you might say, if you knew nothing about
her. If you were sorting through a box of old photographs
in a junk shop and came across this particular sepia, faded
face above the choked collars of the 1890s, you might murmur when you saw her: 'Oh, what big eyes you have!' as
Red Riding Hood said to the wolf, but then you might not
even pause to pick her out and look at her more closely, for
hers is not, in itself, a striking face.

But as soon as the face has a name, once you recognize
her, when you know who she is and what it was she did,
the face becomes as if of one possessed, and now it haunts
you, you look at it again and again, it secretes mystery.

This woman, with her jaw of a concentration-camp
attendant, and such eyes ...

In her old age, she wore pince-nez, and truly with the
years the mad light has departed from those eyes or else is
deflected by her glasses – if, indeed, it *was* a mad light, in
the first place, for don't we all conceal somewhere photographs of ourselves that make us look like crazed assassins?
And, in those early photographs of her young womanhood,
she herself does not look so much like a crazed assassin as
somebody in extreme solitude, oblivious of that camera in
whose direction she obscurely smiles, so that it would not
surprise you to learn that she is blind.

There is a mirror on the dresser in which she sometimes
50 looks at those times when time snaps in two and then she

sees herself with blind, clairvoyant eyes, as though she were another person.

'Lizzie is not herself, today.'

At those times, those irremediable times, she could have raised her muzzle to some aching moon and howled.

At other times, she watches herself doing her hair and trying her clothes on. The distorting mirror reflects her with the queasy fidelity of water. She puts on dresses and then she takes them off. She looks at herself in her corset. She pats her hair. She measures herself with the tape-measure. She pulls the measure tight. She pats her hair. She tries on a hat, a little hat, a chic little straw toque. She punctures it with a hatpin. She pulls the veil down. She pulls it up. She takes the hat off. She drives the hatpin into it with a strength she did not know she possessed.

Time goes by and nothing happens.

She traces the outlines of her face with an uncertain hand as if she were thinking of unfastening the bandages on her soul but it isn't time to do that, yet: she isn't ready to be seen, yet.

She is a girl of Sargasso calm.

She used to keep her pigeons in the loft above the disused stable and feed them grain out of the palms of her cupped hands. She liked to feel the soft scratch of their beaks. They murmured 'vroo croo' with infinite tenderness. She changed their water every day and cleaned up their leprous messes but Old Borden took a dislike to their cooing, it got on his nerves, who'd have thought he *had* any nerves but he invented some, they got on them, one afternoon he took out the hatchet from the woodpile in the cellar and chopped those pigeons' heads right off, he did.

Abby fancied the slaughtered pigeons for a pie but Bridget the servant girl put her foot down, at that: what?!? make a pie out of Miss Lizzie's beloved turtledoves? Jesus Mary and Joseph!!! she exclaimed with characteristic impetuousness, what can they be thinking of! Miss Lizzie so nervy with her funny turns and all! (The maid is the only one in the house with any sense and that's the truth of it.) Lizzie came home from the Fruit and Flower Mission for whom she had been reading a tract to an old woman in a poorhouse: 'God bless you, Miss Lizzie.' At home all was blood and feathers.

She doesn't weep, this one, it isn't her nature, she is still waters, but, when moved, she changes colour, her face flushes, it goes dark, angry, mottled red. The old man loves his daughter this side of idolatry and pays for everything she wants, but all the same he killed her pigeons when his wife wanted to gobble them up.

That is how she sees it. That is how she understands it. She cannot bear to watch her stepmother eat, now. Each bite the woman takes seems to go: 'Vroo croo.'

Old Borden cleaned off the hatchet and put it back in the cellar, next to the woodpile. The red receding from her face, Lizzie went down to inspect the instrument of destruction. She picked it up and weighed it in her hand.

That was a few weeks before, at the beginning of the spring.

Her hands and feet twitch in her sleep; the nerves and muscles of this complicated mechanism won't relax, just won't relax, she is all twang, all tension, she is taut as the strings of a wind-harp from which random currents of the air pluck out tunes that are not our tunes.

At the first stroke of the City Hall clock, the first factory hooter blares, and then, on another note, another, and another, the Metacomet Mill, the American Mill, the Mechanics Mill . . . until every mill in the entire town sings out aloud in a common anthem of summoning and hot alleys where the factory folk live blacken with the hurrying throng: hurry! scurry! to loom, to bobbin, to spindle, to dye-shop as to places of worship, men, and women, too, and children, the streets blacken, the sky darkens as the chimneys now belch forth, the clang, bang, clatter of the mills commences.

Bridget's clock leaps and shudders on its chair, about to sound its own alarm. Their day, the Bordens' fatal day, trembles on the brink of beginning.

Outside, above, in the already burning air, see! the angel of death roosts on the roof-tree.

PENGUIN 60s

ISABEL ALLENDE · *Voices in My Ear*
NICHOLSON BAKER · *Playing Trombone*
LINDSEY BAREHAM · *The Little Book of Big Soups*
KAREN BLIXEN · *From the Ngong Hills*
DIRK BOGARDE · *Coming of Age*
ANTHONY BURGESS · *Childhood*
ANGELA CARTER · *Lizzie Borden*
CARLOS CASTANEDA · *The Sorcerer's Ring of Power*
ELIZABETH DAVID · *Peperonata and Other Italian Dishes*
RICHARD DAWKINS · *The Pocket Watchmaker*
GERALD DURRELL · *The Pageant of Fireflies*
RICHARD ELLMANN · *The Trial of Oscar Wilde*
EPICURUS · *Letter on Happiness*
MARIANNE FAITHFULL · *Year One*
KEITH FLOYD · *Hot and Spicy Floyd*
ALEXANDER FRATER · *Where the Dawn Comes Up like Thunder*
ESTHER FREUD · *Meeting Bilal*
JOHN KENNETH GALBRAITH · *The Culture of Contentment*
ROB GRANT AND DOUG NAYLOR · *Scenes from the Dwarf*
ROBERT GRAVES · *The Gods of Olympus*
JANE GRIGSON · *Puddings*
SOPHIE GRIGSON · *From Sophie's Table*
KATHARINE HEPBURN · *Little Me*
JAMES HERRIOT · *Seven Yorkshire Tales*
SUSAN HILL · *The Badness within Him*
ALAN HOLLINGHURST · *Adventures Underground*
BARRY HUMPHRIES · *Less is More Please*
HOWARD JACOBSON · *Expulsion from Paradise*
P. D. JAMES · *The Girl Who Loved Graveyards*
STEPHEN KING · *Umney's Last Case*

PENGUIN 60s

READ MORE IN PENGUIN

For complete information about books available from Penguin and how to order them, please write to us at the appropriate address below. Please note that for copyright reasons the selection of books varies from country to country.

IN THE UNITED KINGDOM: Please write to *Dept. EP, Penguin Books Ltd, Bath Road, Harmondsworth, Middlesex UB7 0DA.*

IN THE UNITED STATES: Please write to *Consumer Sales, Penguin USA, P.O. Box 999, Dept. 17109, Bergenfield, New Jersey 07621-0120.* VISA and MasterCard holders call 1-800-253-6476 to order Penguin titles.

IN CANADA: Please write to *Penguin Books Canada Ltd, 10 Alcorn Avenue, Suite 300, Toronto, Ontario M4V 3B2.*

IN AUSTRALIA: Please write to *Penguin Books Australia Ltd, P.O. Box 257, Ringwood, Victoria 3134.*

IN NEW ZEALAND: Please write to *Penguin Books (NZ) Ltd, Private Bag 102902, North Shore Mail Centre, Auckland 10.*

IN INDIA: Please write to *Penguin Books India Pvt Ltd, 706 Eros Apartments, 56 Nehru Place, New Delhi 110 019.*

IN THE NETHERLANDS: Please write to *Penguin Books Netherlands bv, Postbus 3507, NL-1001 AH Amsterdam.*

IN GERMANY: Please write to *Penguin Books Deutschland GmbH, Metzlerstrasse 26, 60594 Frankfurt am Main.*

IN SPAIN: Please write to *Penguin Books S. A., Bravo Murillo 19, 1° B, 28015 Madrid.*

IN ITALY: Please write to *Penguin Italia s.r.l., Via Felice Casati 20, I-20124 Milano.*

IN FRANCE: Please write to *Penguin France S. A., 17 rue Lejeune, F-31000 Toulouse.*

IN JAPAN: Please write to *Penguin Books Japan, Ishikiribashi Building, 2-5-4, Suido, Bunkyo-ku, Tokyo 112.*

IN GREECE: Please write to *Penguin Hellas Ltd, Dimocritou 3, GR-106 71 Athens.*

IN SOUTH AFRICA: Please write to *Longman Penguin Southern Africa (Pty) Ltd, Private Bag X08, Bertsham 2013.*